This book belongs to

My friend Lia
love Ava ♥

This edition published by Parragon in 2011

Parragon
Queen Street House
4 Queen Street
Bath BA1 1HE, UK

ISBN 978-1-4454-3317-2

Printed in China

The Perfect Snowflake

Parragon

Bath • New York • Singapore • Hong Kong • Cologne • Delhi
Melbourne • Amsterdam • Johannesburg • Auckland • Shenzhen

One morning, Emma woke up to find
something magical happening outside
her bedroom window.

"It's snowing!" she whispered excitedly, her warm breath making misty patterns on the glass.

Outside, snowflakes swirled and twirled in the air before floating to the ground.

Emma had never seen anything so beautiful.
"If only I could have a snowflake of my
own to keep!" she thought.

In the yard, Emma caught lots of snowflakes, but each one disappeared when she tried to show Mommy.

"Snowflakes melt when they're warm," Mommy explained.

"But I wanted to keep one!" Emma sighed.

Later that day, the sun shone just
as the last few snowflakes fell.
They shimmered in the light
like sparkly diamonds,
before vanishing onto
the ground.

That afternoon, Mommy showed
Emma how to make a paper snowflake.
"It's not the same as having a REAL
snowflake," Emma sighed, remembering
what it was like to play in the snow.

"REAL snowflakes dance in the sky."

"REAL snowflakes sparkle in the sun."

"REAL snowflakes **dazzle** like diamonds in the snow!"

Emma couldn't wait to play with REAL snowflakes again.

But the next morning,
when Emma went outside to
play, all the snow had melted.

Just then, the most
perfect snowflake
Emma had ever seen
fluttered in the sky.

This snowflake **danced** in the sky…

sparkled in the sun, and... dazzled like a diamond.

But this snowflake
wasn't real. It was made
of paper, with sparkly
sequins and glitter
sprinkled on top.

Emma hugged Mommy. "This snowflake is definitely one I can keep," she grinned.

How to make Emma's perfect snowflake:

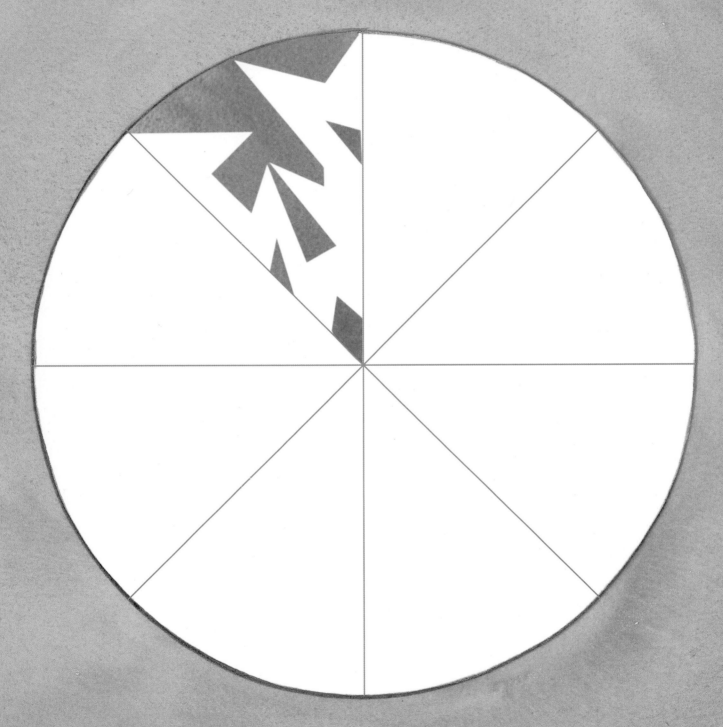

Copy the above pattern onto paper. Ask a grown up to help you cut out the circle, then fold on the black lines, and cut away the purple areas to reveal your snowflake.